big fat hen

ILLUSTRATED BY

KEITH BAKER

HARCOURT BRACE & COMPANY

SAN DIEGO   NEW YORK   LONDON

PRINTED IN SINGAPORE

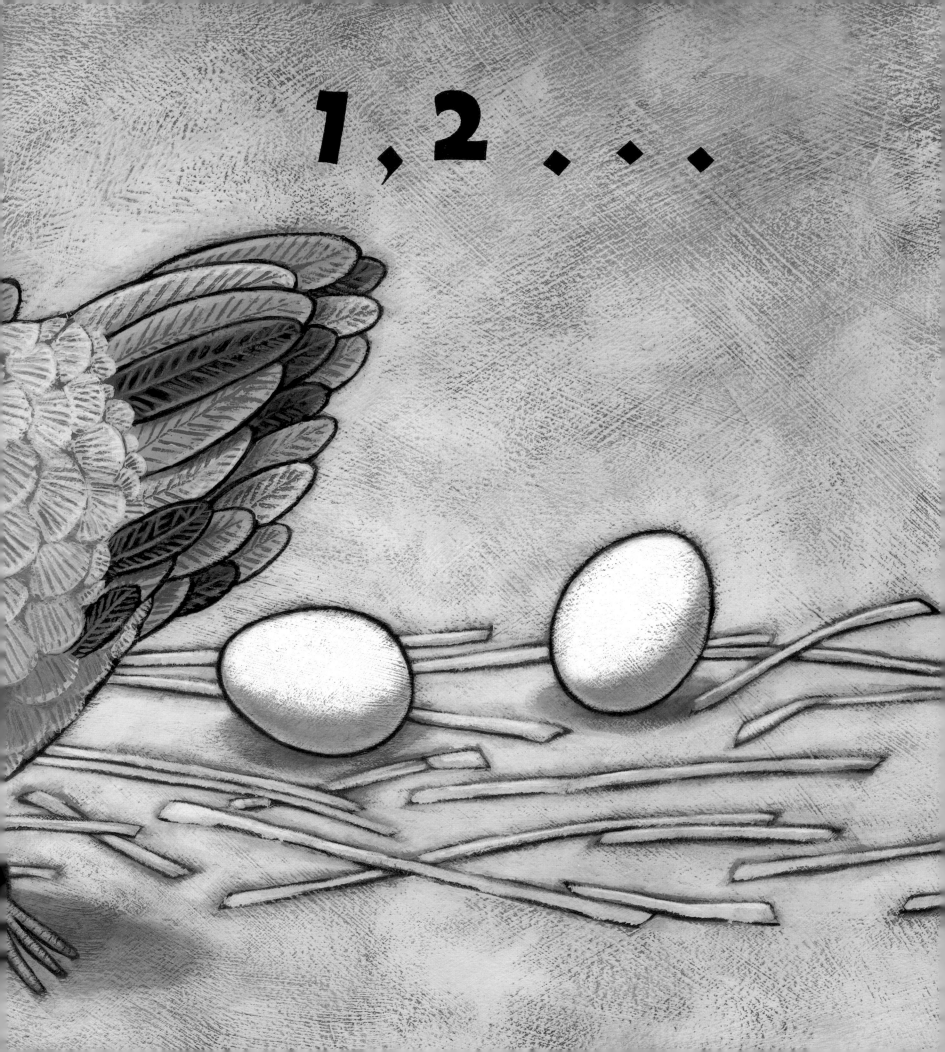

buckle my shoe

shut the door

5, 6 . . .

pick up sticks

lay them straight

9, 10 . . .

a big

fat hen

and

her friends

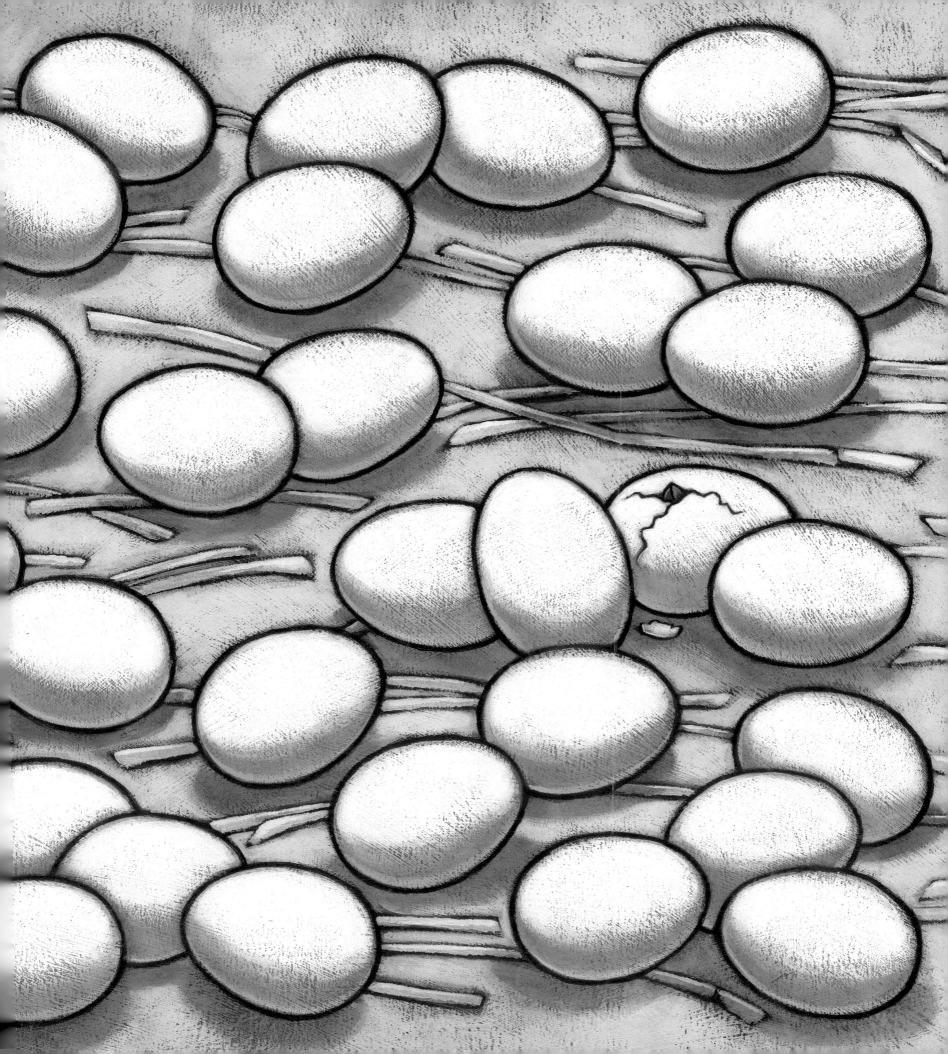

and all their chicks!

Library of Congress Cataloging-in-Publication Data
Baker, Keith, 1953–
Big fat hen/Keith Baker — 1st ed.
p.   cm.
Summary: Big Fat Hen counts to ten
with her friends and all their chicks.
ISBN 0-15-200294-4
1. Nursery rhymes.   2. Children's poetry.
[1. Nursery rhymes.   2. Counting.]   I. Title.
PZ8.3.B175Bi   1994
[E]—dc20   93-19160

Special Edition for Scholastic Book Fairs
A B C D E

The illustrations in this book were done in
Liquitex acrylics on illustration board.
The text and display type was hand-lettered by Georgia Deayer.
Color separations by Bright Arts, Ltd., Singapore
Printed and bound by Tien Wah Press, Singapore
Production supervision by Warren Wallerstein and Kent MacElwee
Designed by Trina Stahl